MR. CLUMSY

by Roger Hargreaves

EGMONT

It was a rather nice morning.

In the sky, the sun was up.

Shining.

In the trees, the birds were up.

Singing.

But, in a rather scruffy house in the middle of a field, somebody wasn't up.

Can you guess who that somebody might be?

His alarm clock went off.

Mr Clumsy woke up, and reached out an arm to switch off his alarm clock.

And knocked it on to the floor.

"Whoops," he said. "That's the third alarm clock I've broken this week."

Mr Clumsy, as you might have guessed, was a rather clumsy fellow.

He got out of bed and switched on the radio.

The knob came off in his hand.

"Whoops," he said. "That's the second radio I've broken this month."

He stumbled down the stairs.

The postman had been, and there was a letter waiting for Mr Clumsy, lying on his doormat.

He picked it up, and went into his kitchen.

"First things first," he said, and took a slice of bread out of his bread bin and popped it into his toaster.

"Now," he thought, "I wonder who this letter is from."

He looked at the letter in his hand.

But the letter wasn't in his hand.

What was in his hand was a slice of bread!

"I don't understand it," he said. "Where's the letter gone?"

Can you guess where the letter had gone?

That's right! He'd put the letter in the toaster instead of the bread!

And there it was, browning nicely.

"Whoops," he said, fishing it out.

"Ouch," he said, dropping it. "It's hot!"

Mr Clumsy bent down to pick the letter up.

But, in doing so, he banged his forehead on his kitchen table and, in doing so, he fell forwards and got his head stuck in the bread bin!

All of which wasn't surprising really.

As we said, he was a rather clumsy fellow.

In fact, he was a very clumsy fellow.

Actually, he was the clumsiest person in the world!

That very same morning, after he'd managed to get the bread bin off his head, Mr Clumsy went to town.

Shopping.

"First things first," he said, and went into the bank to get some money.

And somehow, while he was in the bank, Mr Clumsy, while he was writing a cheque, managed to spill ink all over the bank manager.

"Whoops," said Mr Clumsy.

He went into the butcher's.

"Morning, butcher," he said, cheerily.

And then, he somehow managed to trip over his shoelaces, and somehow managed to fall into the butcher's shop window, and somehow managed to finish up with a string of sausages round his neck!

"Whoops," he said.

Mr Clumsy's next call was the supermarket.

Just inside the door there was a huge pyramid pile of cans of soup.

Well.

You can imagine what happened, can't you?

"Mmm," exclaimed Mr Clumsy. "Soup would be nice for supper," and he picked up a can.

Not a can from the top of the pile.

Oh no, not Mr Clumsy.

"Whoops," said Mr Clumsy, and went on his way.

Rubbing his head.

On his way home, he called in at the farm for some eggs.

And somehow, while he was crossing the farmyard, he managed to trip up.

And somehow, as he was falling, he managed to grab hold of the farmer.

And somehow, they both managed to finish up in the duck pond!

SPLASH!

"Whoops," said Mr Clumsy.

"Please," said the farmer, as they sat together in the duck pond. "In future, can I deliver your eggs to you?"

"That's extraordinarily kind of you," replied Mr Clumsy.

"Don't mention it," muttered the farmer.

Mr Clumsy went home.

"First things first," he said, and went for a bath.

But, as he was stepping into his bath, his foot somehow managed to slip on the soap, and he somehow managed to turn a somersault, and he somehow managed to land with his head in the linen basket.

"Whoops!" said a muffled voice.

Later, he went downstairs for supper.

Soup, from the supermarket.

Sausages, from the butcher's.

And eggs, from the farm.

Or rather.

Soup, from the saucepan that had boiled over.

Sausages, from the frying pan that had caught fire.

And eggs, oh dear, very very very scrambled eggs!

A normal Mr Clumsy sort of supper.

"That was nice," he said, leaning back in his chair.

CRASH!

"Whoops!" said Mr Clumsy. "I think I'd better go to bed."

And he did.

And that is the end of the story.

Good night, Mr Clumsy!

Mr Clumsy leaned over to turn off his bedside light, and …

Oh dear.

"Whoops!"

Fantastic offers for Mr. Men fans!

Only need a few Mr. Men or Little Miss to complete your set? You can order any of the titles on the back of the books from our Mr. Men order line on 0870 787 1724.

The majority of orders are delivered in 5 to 7 working days.

TO BE COMPLETED BY AN ADULT

To apply for any of these great offers, ask an adult to complete the details below and send this whole page with the appropriate payment and tokens, to: MR. MEN CLASSIC OFFER PO BOX 715, HORSHAM RH12 5WG

☐ Please send me a giant-sized double-sided collector's poster.

AND ☐ I enclose 6 tokens and have taped a £1 coin to the other side of this page

---

☐ Please send me ☐ Mr. Men Library case(s) and/or ☐ Little Miss Library case(s) at £5.99 each inc P&P

☐ I enclose a cheque/postal order payable to Egmont UK Limited for £...............

OR ☐ Please debit my MasterCard / Visa / Maestro / Delta account (delete as appropriate) for £...............

Card no. ☐☐☐☐ ☐☐☐☐ ☐☐☐☐ ☐☐☐☐ ☐☐☐☐ Security code ☐☐☐

Issue no. (if available) ☐ Start Date ☐☐ / ☐☐ / ☐☐ Expiry Date ☐☐ / ☐☐ / ☐☐

Fan's name: .... Date of birth: ....

Address: ....

....

.... Postcode: ....

Name of parent / guardian: ....

Email of parent / guardian: ....

Signature of parent / guardian ....

Offer is only available while stocks last. We reserve the right to change the terms of this offer at any time and we offer a 14 day money back guarantee. Please allow up to 28 days for delivery. This does not affect your statutory rights. Offers apply to UK only.

☐ We may occasionally wish to send you information about other Egmont books. If you would rather we didn't please tick this box.